SCOOBY-DOO! AND THE SPOOKY STRIKEOUT

Written by
James Gelsey

A
LITTLE APPLE
PAPERBACK

SCHOLASTIC INC.

New York Toronto London Auckland Sydney
Mexico City New Delhi Hong Kong

For Lew and Jerry

ISBN 0-439-11349-0

30 29 28 27 26 25   7 8 9 10 11 12/0

Printed in the U.S.A.
First Scholastic printing, May 2000

Chapter 1

"**R**one! Rwoo! Ree rikes, rou're rout rat ree rold rall rame!" Scooby sang in the back of the van.

Shaggy wildly applauded Scooby's singing.

"Boy, Shaggy, I didn't know you liked Scooby's singing so much," Fred said.

"Like, I don't," Shaggy replied. "I was clapping because he finally stopped."

Fred steered the Mystery Machine into the parking lot. They could see the baseball stadium straight ahead.

"There it is," Daphne said. "Shakey Field. Home of the Shakey Comets."

"Shaggy, I'm sure glad you won tickets to this game," Fred said. "I love baseball."

"How many pizza pies did you have to eat to win these tickets?" Velma asked.

"Like, only about fifty," Shaggy said.

"Fifty pizzas during one year?" Velma said. "That comes out to about one pizza a week."

"Who said anything about a year?" Shaggy replied. "Like, I ate all fifty pizzas in one month."

"One month?" Daphne exclaimed. "How'd you do that?"

"With a little help from Scooby-Doo, of course," Shaggy said. "It's like I always say: Two stomachs are better than one. Right, Scoob?"

"Right!" Scooby barked.

"Well, I'm just glad we're here," Daphne

said. "Now I have a chance to interview the team's owner for the school paper."

Fred parked the van and the gang got out. Everyone wore baseball caps. Fred put on a Comets baseball jacket. Daphne made sure she had her pad and pen. Velma put a small book into her pocket.

"Velma, we're going to a ball game, not a library," Shaggy said.

"This book is on the physics of baseball," Velma replied. "It explains things like how a curveball works."

"Like, Scooby-Doo and I are more interested in how the snack bar works," Shaggy replied. He and Scooby laughed as the gang walked toward the front gate.

Just outside the gate they saw a man dressed in an old Shakey Comets baseball uniform. He was wearing a big sign around his neck. The sign said BOO COMETS!

"Boo, Comets!" the man yelled. "Tillis Shakey is bad for baseball! Save your money and go home!"

The gang walked right by him and through the gate.

"I guess he's not a fan," Daphne said.

The gang handed their passes to the ticket taker. A security guard came up next to them. He looked at the tickets.

"Come with me, please," the guard said.

"Like, we haven't even made one trip for popcorn and we're in trouble already," Shaggy moaned.

"I don't think we're in trouble," Daphne said.

"Daphne's right," Velma added. "Look."

Everyone looked up and saw a sign in front of them. The sign said VIP'S THIS WAY.

"Man, we're goners for sure," Shaggy said. "They're taking us to the cemetery."

"Cemetery? What are you talking about, Shaggy?" Daphne asked.

"Like, the sign said RIP's," Shaggy replied. "It's what they write on tombstones. Rest in Peace."

"The sign said VIP's, not RIP's," Velma explained. "VIP stands for Very Important Person."

By the time Velma finished explaining, the guard had stopped walking. The gang found themselves in a special section of seats.

"Wow!" Fred gasped. "We're right behind the dugout."

"I hope these seats are okay," a strange voice said. The gang turned around and saw a short, stocky man standing in front of them.

"I'm Tillis Shakey," he said, extending his hand. "Welcome to my stadium."

Chapter 2

The gang's seats were in a special box right alongside the playing field. They could almost reach out and touch the field. They could also see right into the Comets' dugout.

"It's my pleasure to welcome you," Tillis Shakey said. "Now, which one of you ate the fifty pizzas?"

Everyone looked at Shaggy.

"Like, that's me," Shaggy said.

"I am so happy to meet you, uh . . ." Mr. Shakey said.

"Shaggy," Shaggy replied.

"You should know, Shaggy, that I don't usually give these seats away," Mr. Shakey continued. "These are my private seats. I like to be close to the action. But when I heard about the fifty pizzas, I knew I had to do something special." He leaned over to Shaggy. "You see, I love pizza, too," he whispered. "I once ate two whole pies all by myself in one night."

"Groovy," Shaggy replied. "Where's the snack bar?"

"Shaggy!" Daphne scolded. "That wasn't very nice!"

"Oh, that's all right," Mr. Shakey said. "The concessions are up those stairs." He pointed up the long staircase that rose through the stands behind them.

"That's a long way for some snacks," Shaggy said.

"Excuse me, Mr. Shakey," Daphne began. "Are there always so many security guards at a baseball game?"

"Absolutely," Mr. Shakey answered. "We don't want people just wandering around."

"That makes sense," Fred agreed. "But this is a championship game, right?"

Tillis Shakey nodded.

"Then why is the stadium so empty?" Velma asked.

"I can answer that," someone interrupted. The gang looked at the next row of seats. A man folded up his cell phone and put it in his pocket.

"The stadium is so empty because the games are so boring," the man said. "If I owned this team, people would be waiting in line to get in. We'd have something exciting happening at every baseball game."

A ringing sound came from his pocket. The man took out his cell phone. As he talked, he walked up the stairs into the stands.

"Who was that?" Fred asked.

"That was Hubert Hibbert," Mr. Shakey said.

"Doesn't he own that chain of electronics stores?" Daphne said.

"That's right," Mr. Shakey replied. "He has wanted to buy the team for years." Mr. Shakey sighed. "Hubert is right about one thing. Our games *are* boring. And if we don't win this championship, I can probably kiss the Comets good-bye."

"And I think it's time for me and Scoob to kiss our hunger good-bye," Shaggy said.

"Like, we'll see you cats later."

"Be careful, you two," Daphne warned. "Don't get into any trouble."

"Relax, Daphne," Shaggy said. "We're at a baseball game. What kind of trouble could we possibly get into?"

"We don't want to find out," Velma said.

Chapter 3

Shaggy and Scooby started climbing the long flight of stairs. The steps were very steep and seemed to go on forever.

"Like, all this walking is making me hungrier," said Shaggy. "There's gotta be a shortcut around here."

Scooby looked around. He saw a man walk out of a hidden opening beneath the next row of seats. The man was holding a big, square tub with one hand. In the other hand, he was waving a bag of popcorn.

"POP-corn here!" the popcorn man

yelled. "Get yer hot, fresh POP-corn here!"

Scooby had an idea.

"Raggy!" he barked. "Rollow me." Scooby walked toward the opening beneath the seats.

"Like, where're we headed, Scoob?" Shaggy asked. As they got closer, another man walked through the opening. He held a tray of cups around his neck with a big red strap.

"Scooby, old pal, you've outdone yourself this time," Shaggy said. "You've found the back way to the snack way."

They walked through the opening and down a dark tunnel. They followed the smell of the popcorn as the path turned left, then right, then left again. Shaggy and Scooby were soon lost.

"Maybe this wasn't such a good idea," Shaggy said. "Now we're lost and I'm hungrier than ever. What are we going to do?"

Scooby noticed someone standing in the shadows along the wall.

"Rask rim," he said. He pointed at the figure.

"I don't know, Scoob," Shaggy began.

The figure stepped away from the wall. From his shadowy outline, he looked like an umpire.

"Oh, it's just an umpire," Shaggy said. "He'll know which way to go. They know everything." He and Scooby walked over to the figure.

"Like, excuse us, Mr. Umpire," Shaggy said. "Can you tell us the way to the snack bar?"

The figure turned around. It wasn't just any baseball umpire. It was a baseball umpire ghost!

"Zoinks!" Shaggy exclaimed.

"Rikes!" Scooby barked. He jumped into Shaggy's arms.

"Leave this place," the ghostly umpire moaned. "This stadium is cursed. This base-

ball team is cursed. And if you do not leave, then you will be cursed, too!"

"Like, we get the picture, man," Shaggy said. "Let's split, Scoob!" He and Scooby ran back the way they came.

"I don't know about you, Scooby," Shaggy called as he ran. "But I've suddenly lost my appetite."

"Reah, me roo!" Scooby agreed. They followed the tunnel back out to the seats. Daphne was just about to start interviewing Tillis Shakey when Shaggy and Scooby ran over to them.

"Like, you're not gonna believe this," Shaggy said.

"Believe what?" Daphne asked.

"Scooby and I just saw a ghost!" Shaggy said.

"A ghost?" Velma asked. She looked up from her book. "Where did you see a ghost?"

"Like, we were on our way to the snack

bar," Shaggy explained. "We must've taken a wrong turn. Anyway, the next thing we know, this green-masked umpire is telling us the whole place is cursed."

"Green-masked umpire?" Mr. Shakey asked. "I've heard umpires called a lot of things in my day, but never green-masked."

"I'm telling you, man," Shaggy said. "He was at least seven feet tall. Right, Scooby?"

"Reah, rike ris," Scooby said. He stood up on his back legs. He twisted up his face into a scary growl.

"Grrrrrrrrr," he growled.

"That's probably just Lefty Fields," Mr. Shakey said.

"The pitcher?" Fred asked.

"The ex-pitcher," Mr. Shakey continued. "He's mad at me for releasing him from the team."

"Was he the guy wearing that 'Boo Comets!' sign we saw outside?" Daphne asked.

"That was definitely Lefty," Mr. Shakey said. "He'll do anything to scare people away just to get back at me."

"That would explain it, Shaggy," Velma said. "See, there's nothing to worry about."

"Easy for you to say," Shaggy said. "You didn't just have your appetite scared right out of you."

Chapter 4

Daphne checked her notebook one more time.

"Are you ready, Mr. Shakey?" Daphne asked.

"Fire away," he replied.

"Great," she said. "When did you first become involved with the Comets?"

"Well, Daphne, it was about thirty years ago," Mr. Shakey said. "I had just graduated from college, and I —"

"— decided to try out for the Comets," a woman said, finishing his sentence. The gang turned and saw a woman standing right next to their seats. She had bright red hair and wore pointy, blue-rimmed eyeglasses.

"Cindy Newkirk, KCPR television," she said. She reached over and shook Tillis Shakey's hand. "I'm here for an interview for our eleven o'clock sports report."

"That's wonderful," Mr. Shakey replied. "As soon as I'm done with this young lady, I'll be happy to answer your questions. Now then, where was I?"

"Excuse me, Till," Cindy interrupted. "May I call you Till?" She walked over to Mr. Shakey and put her arm around him. She started talking softly, but Daphne could still hear her.

"Now, Till," she began, "I'm with the biggest television station in town. I'm talking to you about the eleven o'clock news. Major coverage of a major sporting event. And

heaven knows your team could use the coverage. So what do you say?"

Mr. Shakey thought for a moment.

"Well, I don't know, Cindy," he said. "This young lady was here first. I won't be long. Thanks for understanding."

Mr. Shakey turned back to Daphne.

"Now you see here, Shakey," Cindy said forcefully. "I can't wait for you to finish with some high school student. If I don't get a real story about this baseball game, I'm going to be back repairing radios and television cameras. So if you're not going to talk to me, I'll find another story around here. Something even bigger than you."

Cindy turned and walked up the stairs in a hurry. On her way up, she bumped into Hubert Hibbert. He was on his way back to his seat.

"What happened, Shakey?" Hubert asked as he sat down. "Was that another unhappy fan storming out of the stadium?"

"That was just some television reporter," Mr. Shakey replied. "I'm sorry you had to hear all that, Daphne."

"Oh, that's all right," Daphne said. "Some people just can't help being rude."

"Or bored," Hubert added. "That's why I invented this." He reached up and took a small black clip off his ear. "It picks up the announcer's comments so you don't have to strain to understand them. And when the games get boring, you can switch it to pick up regular radio stations. Perfect for Comets games. And just the sort of thing that every fan would get at the new Hibbert Comets Stadium."

"All right, Hubert, that's enough," Mr. Shakey said. "I'm not selling."

"We'll see," Hubert replied. "The game hasn't even started yet."

Daphne was about to start asking her next question when the PA system came alive with a crackle of static. "Ladies and gentlemen," the announcer said. "Please rise for the national anthem."

"Looks like the game's about to start, Daphne," Mr. Shakey said. "What do you say we do this interview between innings?"

"That's fine, Mr. Shakey," Daphne said.

"Good," he replied. "Then let's watch some baseball!"

Chapter 5

After the national anthem ended, the home plate umpire yelled, "Play ball!"

The Shakey Comets ran out onto the field and took their positions. The pitcher threw a few warm-up pitches. Then the first batter from the Coleman Knights stepped up to the plate.

The first pitch sailed right over the plate. *Whoosh!*

"Stee-rike!" the umpire called.

The second pitch came in at the same angle. The batter swung the bat. *CRACK!* The ball flew into the air over the field. The outfielder ran back, back, back up to the fence. He looked up and watched the ball crash into the scoreboard. The crowd cheered. But then the word *Beware* flashed on the scoreboard. Spooky music filled the stadium. The crowd gasped.

The second batter walked up to the plate. He nervously looked around. The pitcher threw the ball. The batter swung. As his bat hit the ball, the bat turned to dust and fell to the ground. The crowd was silent. A spooky green face appeared on the giant television screen next to the scoreboard.

"Like, that's the ghost!" Shaggy exclaimed.

Scooby took one look and then slid under his seat to hide.

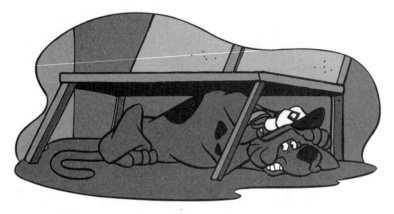

"This stadium is cursed," the voice said. "This game is cursed. And if you remain, then all of you will be cursed, too." The image faded as the umpires got together on the field.

Velma noticed Hubert Hibbert making a call on his cell phone and then touching his ear radio.

The home plate umpire motioned for the game to resume. The batter nervously returned to the plate. He held his bat carefully and not too tightly. The pitcher threw a fastball right over the plate. The batter swung and made contact. *POP!*

But instead of sailing out over the field, the ball broke apart. A real, live bat flew out and over the batter's head. He ducked and ran into the dugout. Then a whole flock of bats flew out from the scoreboard and around the stadium.

Everyone in the stadium started screaming. They jumped up from their seats and ran toward the exits. The players ran off the field. The stadium emptied. Tillis Shakey couldn't believe his eyes. A man wearing a Comets uniform walked out of the dugout and over to Mr. Shakey.

"Who's that?" Daphne asked.

"That's Red Burney," Mr. Shakey replied. "He's the manager."

"Well, boss, what's the good word?" Red asked.

"I don't think I have any good words, Red," Mr. Shakey replied.

"I do," Hubert Hibbert said. "How about, 'Name your price, Hubert.'" Hubert Hibbert smiled and walked away.

"That won't be necessary, Mr. Shakey," Fred said.

"Why not?" Mr. Shakey asked.

"Because the Mystery, Inc. gang is on the case," Fred replied. "Just leave everything to us."

Chapter 6

"The first thing we need to do is split up to look for clues," Fred stated.

Velma nodded in agreement. "Right," she said. "Why don't you and Daphne go with Mr. Shakey to check out the announcer's booth and inside the stadium?"

"Great idea, Velma," Fred said. "Where will you go?"

"If it's all right with Mr. Burney," Velma began, "I'd like to take a closer look at the ball field and the scoreboard."

"Fine with me, little lady," Red said.

"I guess that leaves me and Scooby," Shaggy said. "Like, we'll go check out the snack bar. Even ghosts get hungry." He and Scooby turned to leave.

"Not so fast, you two," Velma said. "You're coming with me."

"Let's meet back here as soon as we can," Fred said. He and Daphne followed Tillis Shakey up the steps.

"This way, folks," Red Burney said. He turned and walked over to the dugout. Velma, Shaggy, and Scooby hopped over the rail and followed Red onto the field.

Shaggy stopped at home plate and pointed to something on the ground.

"I guess this is all that's left of the bat that turned to dust," he said.

Red Burney knelt down and grabbed some of the dust in his fingers.

"Sawdust," he said.

"And look over here," Velma called. She was about halfway between home plate and the pitcher's mound. She pointed to two pieces of a baseball lying on the ground. Red Burney came over and had a look.

"Looks like someone cut open a real baseball and scooped out the insides," he said.

"Then they put a bat in and only put enough stitches back in to keep it together," Velma continued. "Very interesting. I have a hunch we'll find some answers at the equipment rack. Where can we find it, Mr. Burney?"

"In the dugout," he replied.

"Then let's go," Velma said. "Shaggy, Scooby, you two look for anything else that looks suspicious on the field."

Velma and Red Burney walked back to the dugout. Shaggy and Scooby looked around the field.

"Like, is this groovy or what?" Shaggy asked. "Here we are on a real, live baseball field!"

"Reah," Scooby agreed. "Ret's ro!" He ran onto the pitcher's mound.

"I read you loud and clear, pal," Shaggy said. He ran over to home plate. "Batter up!" he called.

Shaggy stood at the plate. He dug his feet into the dirt. Then he raised a baseball bat up in the air. He took a couple of practice swings. Then he lowered his head and glared at Scooby.

Scooby squinted his eyes and pretended to watch an imaginary catcher. Scooby nodded and went into his windup. He raised his left leg, put it down, reached back with his right arm, and then threw a baseball he had found on the field.

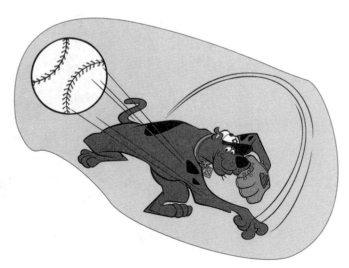

Shaggy swung his bat and started running to first base. Scooby looked up in the air. The ball was coming right at him. As he looked up, Scooby ran toward first base.

Shaggy saw Scooby running and slid into first base. A big cloud of dust flew into the air

as Shaggy got to the base at the same time. When the dust cleared, Shaggy and Scooby looked up. Standing right in front of them was the ghostly umpire.

"You're out!" the ghost yelled.

Shaggy and Scooby jumped up in the air.

"Zoinks!" Shaggy exclaimed. "The ghost!"

He and Scooby turned and ran toward the dugout.

"Velma!" they called.

Chapter 7

Inside the dugout, Velma and Red Burney were looking at the bat rack.

"I make sure every piece of equipment is in place before each game," Red explained.

Just then, Shaggy and Scooby came running over.

"Velma! We saw him! He's right there," Shaggy exclaimed.

"Saw who?" Velma asked.

"The gumpire ohst," Shaggy said. "I mean, the umpire ghost. He's right there at first base and ready to throw me and Scooby out!"

Velma and Red looked at the field.

"Shaggy, there's no one there," Velma said.

"But Scooby and I saw him," Shaggy said. "Right, Scoob?"

"Reah," Scooby agreed. "Rike ris." Scooby stood up on his hind legs. He turned his baseball cap around and made a mean face. "Rou're rout!" he barked.

"If you and Scooby aren't going to help me look for clues," Velma began, "then please sit down and be quiet." She turned around to talk to Red Burney.

"Like, Scooby and I know when we're not wanted," Shaggy said. "Let's go grab that snack, Scoob." He and Scooby turned to leave the dugout. As Scooby walked up the steps, he tripped on something and fell down.

"You okay, Scoob?" Shaggy asked.

"Ri rink ro," Scooby answered.

Shaggy looked at the steps and saw something sticking out of a crack in the cement. He reached down and pulled a bat out of a hole in the step.

"Hey, Velma, look at this," Shaggy said. "Scooby-Doo and I just found a clue."

Red Burney came over and looked at the bat.

"Why, that's Duffy's bat," he said.

"Who's Duffy?" Velma asked.

"The fella whose bat turned to sawdust," Red replied. "But how did his bat get in here?"

Velma bent down and picked up a torn piece of paper. She examined it closely.

"I have a pretty good idea how," Velma said.

"And I have a pretty good idea of my own," Fred said from outside the dugout. He and Daphne walked down the steps.

"What did you find?" Velma asked.

"Take a look at this," Fred said. Daphne held out a small electronic device. It was about the size of a cell phone and had lots of buttons on it.

"It's some kind of remote control device," Daphne said.

"We found it in one of the service tunnels under the seats," Fred explained. "Not too far from where Shaggy and Scooby saw the umpire ghost."

"Like, the first time we saw the ghost?" Shaggy asked.

"Does that mean there's been a second time?" Daphne said.

"I'll tell you one thing," Velma said. "I have a hunch that the third time anyone sees that umpire ghost he's going to strike out."

"You're right, Velma," Fred said. "Gang, it's time to set a trap."

Chapter 8

"The only way we're going to unmask that umpire ghost is to make him think that the baseball game is continuing," Fred said.

"So everyone's going to have to pitch in," Velma said.

"Hey, Velma, like, you just made a joke," Shaggy said. "Everyone has to *pitch* in. Get it? Pitch in? At a baseball game?"

Shaggy and Scooby started giggling.

"This is no time for joking around, you two," Velma said. "There's a ghost out there and we need to catch him."

"And Scooby-Doo's going to help us do it," Fred said.

"Ruh-uh," Scooby barked. "Rot me."

"All you have to do, Scoob," Fred explained, "is to distract the umpire ghost when he shows up."

"Like, nothing to it, pal," Shaggy said.

"Then Shaggy and I will do the rest," Fred continued.

"I was afraid of that," Shaggy moaned.

"What do you say, Scooby," Velma asked. "Will you do it for a Scooby Snack?"

Scooby sat down and turned his head away.

"How about two Scooby Snacks?" Daphne asked.

Scooby started whistling "Take Me Out to the Ball Game."

"How about two Scooby Snacks and a bag of popcorn?" Shaggy asked.

Scooby jumped up.

"Rokay!" he barked.

Daphne took two Scooby Snacks from her pocketbook and tossed them to Scooby. He gobbled them down in one giant gulp. Velma bought a bag of popcorn and Scooby dumped the whole thing in his mouth.

"Now, let's get to work," Fred said. "I'll go find Mr. Burney. Let's go update Mr. Shakey and then get the team together. We'll need them on the field. Shaggy and Scooby, you wait here."

"While you're doing that, Fred," Velma said, "Daphne and I are going to follow another lead."

"Great," Fred replied. "We'll meet back here as quickly as possible."

Fred, Daphne, and Velma walked away. Shaggy and Scooby looked at each other and then at the ball field.

"Are you thinking what I'm thinking, Scoob?" Shaggy asked.

"Ri rink ro," Scooby said with a smile.

They ran back onto the field and picked up a ball.

"Let's get one more play in before everyone gets back," Shaggy said.

This time Shaggy went to the pitcher's

mound. Scooby took his place at home plate. He picked up a bat and got ready to swing. Shaggy reached his arm back, kicked up his leg, and threw a pitch.

"Stee-rike!" a voice shouted. Scooby turned and saw the umpire ghost standing behind home plate.

"Rikes!" Scooby yelled.

"Here we go again!" Shaggy moaned. "Run, Scooby!"

Scooby started running toward first base.

The umpire ghost chased him. Scooby ran around all the bases with the umpire ghost close behind. At one point, the ghost reached out and almost grabbed Scooby's tail.

"Quick, Scoob," Shaggy called. "Into the dugout!"

Shaggy ran across home plate toward the dugout. But as he ran, he bumped into the

bat rack. All of the bats spilled onto the ground.

Scooby slid along the rolling bats toward the other end of the dugout. The umpire ghost ran after Scooby but didn't see the bats. He slipped and slid on the rolling bats so fast he was thrown into the air. The umpire ghost landed on the ground with a thud!

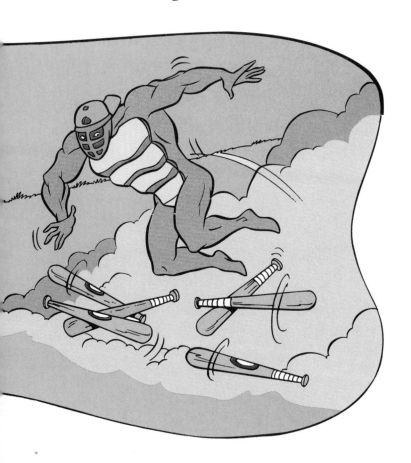

Chapter 9

Shaggy came running toward the dugout. Fred, Daphne, Velma, Red Burney, Tillis Shakey, and the Shakey Comets were right behind him. Red Burney and one of the ballplayers pulled the umpire ghost into the dugout.

"Like, Scooby-Doo, where are you?" Shaggy called.

"Rover rere," Scooby barked. Shaggy followed Scooby's voice and found his friend buried under a pile of baseball bats.

"Are you all right, Scoob?" Shaggy asked.

"Reah," Scooby replied.

Shaggy helped Scooby up. They walked back into the dugout.

"Now, let's go see who's under the umpire's mask," Daphne said. "Would you care to do the honors, Mr. Shakey?"

Tillis Shakey reached out and lifted off the umpire's mask.

"Cindy Newkirk!" Mr. Shakey exclaimed.

"Just as we suspected," Velma said.

"But how did you know?" Mr. Shakey asked.

"We weren't sure at first," Fred said. "Lefty Fields was really our first suspect."

"But with all this security," Velma explained, "an ex-Comet like Lefty would never be able to get around Shakey Field to do all these things."

"So that left Hubert Hibbert and Cindy Newkirk," Daphne said. "They were the only other people who wanted something exciting to happen during the game."

"Then we found the remote control device in the announcer's booth," Fred said. "It looked like just the kind of thing you could find in an electronics store."

"Like the stores that Mr. Hibbert owns," Daphne said.

"But like Lefty Fields," Velma added, "he didn't have access to the field and other places around the stadium."

"The clue that tipped us off was this," Fred said. He held out a torn piece of paper.

"We found this in the dugout right next to the bat rack," Velma explained.

"Why, that's a press pass," Mr. Shakey said. "Or part of one at least."

"That's right," Fred replied. "The same kind of press pass that Cindy Newkirk was wearing when she came to interview you."

"But why?" Mr. Shakey asked. Everyone looked at Cindy.

"Why?" Cindy asked. "Because I needed a big story to save my job. I wasn't about to go back to repairing videotape equipment in the back of the TV station."

"So you did all of this?" Mr. Shakey asked. "Cindy had access to the entire ballpark with her press pass," Daphne said.

"So when she had the chance," Velma continued, "she walked to the dugout and changed the baseball equipment."

"And she rigged up the video player and scoreboard before anyone else got here," Fred added.

"And I would've gotten away with it all if it wasn't for those kids and their meddling mutt," Cindy growled.

"Yeah, yeah," Red Burney said. "That's enough of you. Bring her to the security station, fellas." Two of the baseball players helped Cindy stand up and the three followed Red Burney out of the dugout.

A short while later, the baseball game resumed. The whole gang watched the game from Tillis's box seats. The Shakey Comets won the championship! At the end of the game, the announcer's voice boomed over the loudspeakers.

"Ladies and gentlemen," he said. "Let's hear it for the hero of the day!"

Scooby-Doo's face appeared on the giant TV screen.

Thousands of fans in the stadium stood up and cheered, "Scooby-Dooby-Doo!"

"Awwwwwwww," Scooby said as he blushed with pride.

"That's my pal!" Shaggy exclaimed. "The MVD: Most Valuable Dog!"

About the Author

As a boy, James Gelsey used to run home from school to watch the Scooby-Doo cartoons on television (only after finishing his homework). Today, he still enjoys watching them with his wife and two daughters. He also has a real dog named Scooby who loves nothing more than a good Scooby Snack!

Solve a Mystery With Scooby-Doo!

SCOOBY DOO! MYSTERIES

by James Gelsey

Read them all!

Ruh-roh!

$3.99 each!

Zoinks!